P9-DDL-315

The Sailor's Alphabet

❥ *Illustrated by* Michael McCurdy ❦

Houghton Mifflin Company Boston 1998

E
MCC

For my friend and colleague Robert Hauser, Conservator of the New Bedford Whaling Museum,
whose knowledge of ships was invaluable in the making of this book.

Thanks to James Cheevers, Associate Director and Senior Curator
of the United States Naval Academy Museum, for his inestimable help and guidance.

Thanks also to Robert Webb, Curator, Maine Maritime Museum, for his assistance with maritime terms.

—M. McC.

The text of this book is set in Adobe Caslon.
The illustrations are scratchboard, hand tinted with watercolors.

Library of Congress Cataloging-in-Publication Data

McCurdy, Michael.
The sailor's alphabet / illustrated by Michael McCurdy.
p. cm.
Summary: One of many variations of a forecastle chantey created
about 1837 by an unknown sailor and named after the bow section of
the ship where sailors sometimes bunked or relaxed.
ISBN 0-395-84167-4
1. English language—Alphabet—Juvenile poetry. 2. Seafaring
life—Juvenile poetry. 3. Children's poetry, American. 4. Seamen—
Juvenile poetry. [1. Seafaring life—Poetry. 2. Seamen—Poetry.
3. American poetry. 4. Alphabet.] I. Title.
PS3563.C35317S25 1998
811'.54—dc21   97-20647
CIP AC

Manufactured in the United States of America
HOR 10 9 8 7 6 5 4 3 2 1

❧ Preface ❧

In the age before steam engines and machines, workers toiled with their muscles to build America. This work might have consisted of raising sails, hauling up a ship's anchor, driving railroad spikes, or cutting down trees. Often the labor demanded rhythmical movement, and people would sing songs as they worked, not only to relieve their boredom, but also to make certain everybody kept in time with one another.

Sailors sang songs called sea chanteys. The word chantey probably came from the French word *chanter*—meaning "to sing." Sometimes the word is spelled "chanty," "shantey," or "shanty." There were halyard chanteys, capstan chanteys, whaling chanteys, and forecastle chanteys, among others. (Two of the best-known sea chanteys are "Blow the Man Down" and "Haul Away, Joe.")

The Sailor's Alphabet is a forecastle chantey, named for the bow, or forward, section of the ship, where the sailors sometimes bunked or relaxed when they could. Forecastle chanteys were often filled with nonsense and humor, love or sadness, heroes and adventure. *The Sailor's Alphabet* was created sometime in the 1800s by an unknown sailor and has many variations.

Oh, **A** is the anchor and that you all know,

ANCHOR: A heavy cast-iron object attached to a ship by cable or rope and thrown overboard to keep the vessel from drifting, either by its weight or by its flukes, which grip the bottom.

B is the bowsprit that's over the bow,

BOWSPRIT: A large tapered pole extending forward from the bow of a ship, to which the foremost stays are connected. Attached to the bowsprit is the jib boom, to which the jib sails are secured.

C is the capstan with which we heave 'round,

CAPSTAN: A large, spool-shaped winch on a ship's deck that is used for hauling up sails or anchors. It is turned by sailors using capstan bars.

And **D** are the decks where our sailors are found.

DECK: The flooring covering a ship's hold. Sections of the upper deck include the forecastle, waist (where the sailors are allowed to spend free time), and the quarterdeck (where the officers stand watch).

Oh, **E** is the ensign our mizzen peak flew,

ENSIGN: A national flag displayed on a ship, in this case the American flag. The "mizzen peak" is the very top of the mizzen mast, the farthest mast to the stern, or rear, of a ship.

F is the fo'c'sle where we muster our crew,

FO'C'SLE (forecastle): The foredeck of a ship, a raised platform at the bow, that at one time resembled a castle. In some ships it is the crew's living quarters.

G are the guns, sir, by which we all stand,

GUNS: Before the Civil War, shipboard cannons for naval men-of-war were mostly cast-iron, unrifled twenty-four-pounders. Another cannon, a stumpy carronade called "the smasher," was used for close range.

And **H** are the halyards that ofttimes are manned.

HALYARD (originally "haul yard"): Any rope or tackle used for raising or lowering a sail, yard, spar, or flag.

Oh, **I** is the iron of our stunsail boom sheet,

IRON: An iron spar that is attached to a yard on which a studdingsail ("stunsail") is hung. A "sheet" is any rope used to attach any sails, in this case to attach the stunsail to the iron.

J is the jib that weathers the bleat,

JIB: A triangular sail projecting ahead of the foremast and attached to the jib boom. "Bleat" is another word for blast, as in a blast of wind.

K is the keelson away down below,

KEELSON: A longitudinal beam fastened above and parallel to the keel of a ship to add strength.

And **L** are the lanyards that give us good hold.

LANYARD: Any short rope or cord used on board ship for holding or fastening something. As navies developed, it was also the name of the cord a sailor used to trip the firing mechanism on a ship's cannon.

M is our mainmast so stout and so strong,

MAINMAST: The principal mast of a sailing ship, in most cases the second mast in from the ship's bow.

N is the needle that never points wrong,

NEEDLE: The needle of the ship's compass, used to determine direction and situated near the wheel.

O are the oars of our jolly boat's crew,

OARS: Long wooden poles with broad, thin blades at one end, used in rowing a boat. A "jolly boat" is a ship's small boat.

And **P** is the pennant of red, white, and blue.

PENNANT (originally "pendant"): A long, narrow, tapered flag flown from a mast, sometimes used to designate a military ship or to identify a commanding officer on board.

Q is the quarterdeck where our captain oft stood,

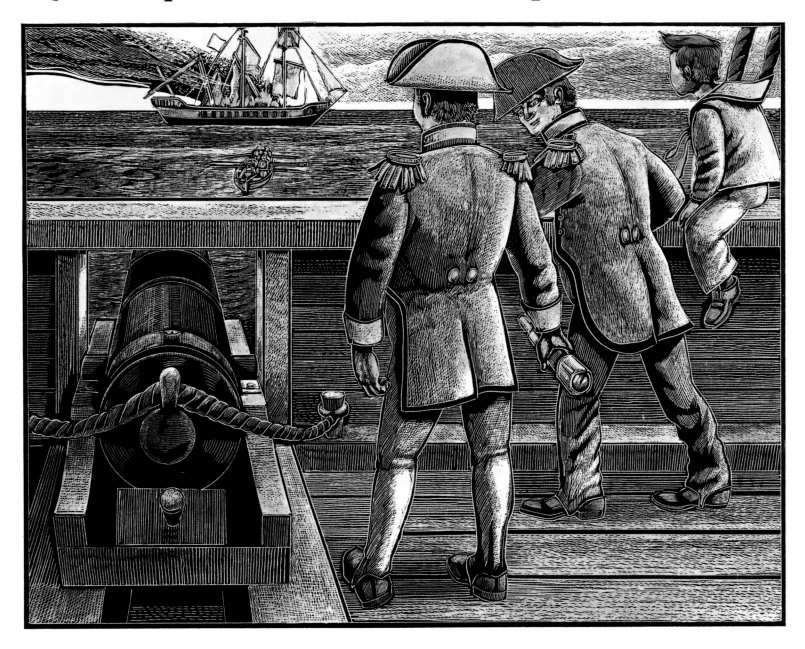

QUARTERDECK: A portion of the upper deck, originally between the poop deck and the mainmast, reserved for ship's officers.

R is the rigging that ever holds good,

RIGGING: All the various ropes, lines, and chains used to support and work the masts, sails, and yards of a ship.

S are the stilliards that weigh out our beef,

STILLIARD (from the word "steelyard"): A scale for weighing objects that has a metal arm suspended off-center from above. An object is hung on the shorter part of the arm, and a sliding weight is moved along the longer end until the whole arm is balanced.

And **T** are the topsails we ofttimes do reef.

TOPSAILS: In a square-rigged ship, the sails just above the lowest sails on a mast. To "reef" a sail is to reduce its size by rolling it and tying it down so it is less exposed to the wind.

Oh, **U** is the Union at which none dare laugh,

UNION: The device in a flag symbolizing union, such as the field of stars in the American flag.

V are the vangs that steady the gaff,

VANGS: Two ropes running from the end of a gaff to the deck. A gaff is a pole extending from a mast and supporting a sail.

W's the wheel that we all take in time,

WHEEL: The wheel is used for steering the ship by means of a system of ropes that pull on the tiller.

And **X** is the letter for which we've no rhyme.

Oh, **Y** are the yards that we ofttimes do brace,

YARDS: Slender spars, tapering toward the ends, that are fastened at right angles across a ship's mast to support a sail. To "brace" a yard is to swing the yard horizontally in order to best catch the wind by pulling on a brace (rope) joined to the ends of each yard.

Z is the letter for which we've no place,
The bos'n pipes grog, so we'll all go below,
My song it is finished, I'm glad that it's so.

Z: "Bo'sn" refers to the boatswain, a petty officer in charge of the crew, who would use a "pipe" to announce, among other things, the serving of "grog" (originally a mixture of rum diluted with water). A pipe is a small whistlelike instrument capable of producing a couple of notes.

A is for anchor

B is for bowsprit

C is for capstan

D is for decks

E is for ensign

F is for fo'c'sle

G is for guns

H is for halyards

I is for iron

J is for jib

K is for keelson

L is for lanyards

M is for mainmast

N is for needle

O is for oars

P is for pennant

Q is for quarterdeck

R is for rigging

S is for stilliards

T is for topsails

U is for Union

V is for vangs

W is for wheel

Y is for yards

✤ Illustrator's Note ✤

The ship illustrated in this book is a United States Navy frigate. Though a frigate is usually the name for a kind of warship, frigates didn't begin as warships. They first sailed the Mediterranean Sea as merchant ships, until the English Royal Navy began using them in the 1500s. The first British frigate designed for war was built in 1652.

Frigates were called the "eyes of the fleet" because they were faster than the earlier, slower-moving "ships of the line." Ships of the line would arrange themselves in a single row and deliver deadly broadsides from their many rows of cannons. Frigates usually had three masts and only one row of cannons on a lower deck. They acted as scouts for the bigger warships. Lone wolves, they were well armed and suited for independent action.

The twenty-six stars on the American flag on this ship serve to place the story about 1837. At this time there were sixteen active frigates in the navy, and pirates were still a menace in the Caribbean. (In 1839, a pirate brig was even captured by the navy off the shores of New London, Connecticut!)